MW00977934

CHRISTMAS COAL

By P. E. Pence

Cover art and Design by P. E. Pence

With illustrations by

Renada Stafford

Copyright 12-16-2016 by P. E. Pence

All Rights Reserved

Any use of this book and its content or characters for personal or commercial use without written permission is prohibited. This is a work of fiction; any similarity of characters, names, places, or incidents, is strictly coincidental, and not meant to be associated with any actual person, place, or event.

New Cover art printed 6-12-2023

ISBN #: 978-1-5202147-1-9

Dedication

*

This

short story

Is dedicated to

Delbert Henry and

Lois Carlyn Hall because

of their love of people and desire

to serve.

CHRISTMAS COAL

Cole sat in the cellar corner facing the wall.

It was not his first time in the corner. In the orphanage, you spend a lot of time in the corner when you choose not to obey rules or be kind to others.

Haunting strains of a violin playing outside the window gave him a chill. He did not understand why he was feeling a chill when he was sitting in the hottest place in the building. Still, there was something eerily familiar about the melody, evoking vague images of a faraway time and place.

Cole turned to see the coal-burning furnace warming the old building on this cold December day. It was almost Christmas, and he knew he would find a lump of coal in his stocking again this year.

"Coal is not so bad," Cole mumbled as he turned to face the wall again. "It's good for lots of things if you have enough of it."

"We are all coal," a voice said.

Cole, startled, jumped upright in his seat and looked around to see who had heard him.

A thin man, blackened by the coal, sat his violin case down and began warming his hands by the stove, then commenced singing words to the melody Cole had heard from the violin moments before;

"A lump of coal can warm you on a cold winter night. Its embers' golden glow makes cozy firelight.

Deep within the earth, where heat and pressure rein,

a coal becomes a diamond, a lovely
precious gem.

We are all coal; we are all coal,
a lump or a diamond, what e 'er is your
goal.

You can just be a cold lump if that is
what you choose,
hide in a corner, feeling lost and abused.

Self-pity and anger deep down in your
soul,
a cold lump or a diamond, you are the
coal.

We are all coal; we are all coal,
a lump or a diamond; what e 'er is your
goal.''

The frail man stopped singing and spoke.

"Spend a lot of time here in the cellar corner, do ya? "

"Yeah, so what if I do? What are you doing here anyway?" Snapped Cole.

"Just warming myself by this fire. Great stuff, coal." The man began singing his song again.

When done singing, he spoke in a heavy Irish accent, "I have a question for you; what can you do with a lump of coal?"

Cole fidgeted in his chair, looking away from the stranger for a moment, then turning back to answer; the stranger was gone.

As the boy sat silently in the corner reflecting, the tune of the stranger's song came into his head, and he began to hum it to himself. Next, the words came, and he began to sing softly as he remembered them. While pondering and singing, Cole started to think of how he had been feeling and how he had grown tired of always being in trouble and seeing the sad eyes of the children and the staff whenever he acted out his anger. He felt especially bad at the tears of the small boy, Henry, who wept whenever Cole was sent to the cellar.

"What does coal do?" he queried to himself. The answer came into his mind as he sang the song. It gives warmth and light, he thought and can become a beautiful diamond.

The hour passed quickly, and soon the orphanage nurse, Nancy, came to tell Cole he could come for supper. She stopped to shovel some coal into the fat-bellied furnace.

Cole quickly held his hands out for the shovel. Nancy curtsied playfully and handed it to him with a smile, and Cole began to fill the stove himself. Being large for a twelve-year-old, it was no trouble for him, and a good feeling came over him the like he had never felt before. Before long, he began to garner a smile all his own!

In the dining hall, Cole sought out Henry, helped him get his food, then sat with him and told jokes and stories that made him laugh. Henry wasn't sure what to make of this change, but he wasn't about to argue or ask why. From that day on, Cole made sure to include Henry in everything he did, and he could tell it made them both happier.

When Christmas came a few days later, there was still a familiar lump of coal in his stocking.

But instead of feeling angry, Cole was happy to have it. It reminded him of what he had been and could become, and he had an idea.

The orphanage was situated on a prominent corner of the town where many people passed each day. Cole secured an old board and some paint and made a sign that said, "Donate the lumps of coal from your stocking." He set an old bucket next to it and waited.

People passed by and smiled at his sign, and soon some came back with a lump or two and even a sack full. Cole had to empty his bucket several times throughout the day.

That winter, the orphanage stayed especially warm as Cole, with his little friend Henry, worked together to keep the old coal stove full. Then spring came, and the summer and the year passed happily as Cole played with the children and helped them with their schoolwork.

He was especially thoughtful of Nurse Nancy and often sat with the sick children to give her time for other things.

Cole and Henry took special care of Michael. In the past, he had spent his days sitting in front of the window watching the seasons change, but now they took turns racing him through the halls in his wheelchair and would spin and whirl him until he squealed with glee.

The following Christmas, Cole's stocking was full to overflowing with treats and small toys, but again there was a lump of coal, not as a sign of misdeeds but a reminder of what you could do with a lump of coal. It was the same for the next year and the next.

At 15, Cole was well loved, not only by the children and staff of the orphanage but many of the people of the town who had been recipients of his warm smile and kind deeds. The winter of his 16th year was bitter cold, so Cole and Henry had to be extra vigilant, keeping the stove stoked.

Once again, it was Christmas Eve. Henry, who wanted so much to do something for his best friend, knew Cole liked the gifts of service best of all, and since he had no money, that suited Henry just fine. Instead of going on the highly anticipated outing with the rest of the children, Henry spent his evening doing some of the chores Cole was leaving for later that night when he would return from spreading Christmas cheer.

The happy sound of children coming in for the night alerted Henry that Cole would be in the midst of the bustle, so he ran to do his last chore, feeding the hungry stove in the cellar. As he thrust in the previous shovel full, Henry heard Cole calling him from upstairs. Hastily, he pushed at the hot door of the stove and ran to the stairs to join the others for cocoa before bed.

Cole was happy to be able to go to bed earlier than he had thought, and

Henry had that good feeling that he had heard Cole talk about so often. The two friends shared a smile and embrace, then left each other to turn in for the night.

The warm rooms and busy, happy day made it easy for everyone to drop off to sleep and sleep soundly... so sound that no one noticed the smell of smoke as it made its way up from the cellar where a clinker had escaped from the stove door. Earlier that evening, Henry, in a rush, had not stopped to shut it tight.

Before anyone awoke to sound an alarm, the whole cellar and lower floor were in flames. Cole frantically corralled a group of children and ushered them out a narrow passage to the outside. After seeing them to safety, he surveyed the situation. "Not all of the children will be able to make it out that way." He thought.

Cole went back in again and again, calling through the corridors and checking each room. For some, he feared there was no way out. Windows painted shut from years of painting had to be broken, and locked doors busted in. The rusty old fire escape would not lower to the ground below. Each time Cole emerged from the burning building, his face grew blacker, and burns were noticed on his limbs and face.

By the time the fire truck arrived, the fire was out of control, daring anyone to re-enter its domain.

"Is everyone out?" Yelled the Fire chief.

Nurse Nancy and the staff frantically counted the children as each one coughed out a weak "here,"; their little lungs burning from the effects of the thick smoke.

"Michael, where is Michael?" she cried out in horror.

Cole threw a wool blanket over his head, burst past the firefighters, and disappeared through smoke and flame.

Anxious minutes passed without hope of seeing the boys again.

"There... On the roof." Yelled the Fire chief.

Cole stood charred and choking at the edge of the parapet, cradling young Michael in his arms.

The firemen grabbed a large, heavy canvas tarp and stretched it taught. Distressed yells came from the crowd below. "Jump! They yelled.

As Cole crouched to leap, the once thick brick wall below him shuddered and collapsed inward. With all the strength he had left, Cole thrust Michael out of his embrace and into the safety of *the net. The firemen quickly withdrew, pushing the crowd back. The heavy brick walls and slate roof fell inward, burying all hope of finding the courageous young man alive.*

Christmas morning came early. Henry had not slept. Wrapped in a thin blanket and with a tear-stained face, he searched alongside the firefighters. Numb and apprehensive, afraid of what he would find, he could not keep himself from looking for evidence, even the slimmest chance of finding his dear friend.

After agonizing hours of searching through piles of brick and ash, Henry wandered to the center of the rubble. Sniffling and snubbing, he began to pick through the debris, stumbling upon the metal remains of the old coal stove. Charred black and lying tilted on its side, the door he had carelessly failed to secure squeaked as it swung freely in the cold morning wind mocking his pain.

The lump in his throat began to tighten and choke his airway. Warm tears fell from his cold cheeks raising tiny plumes of soot as they touched the ashen ground, exposing a glistening object caught in the colorful fractal rays of the sun. Bending down and brushing aside more debris, Henry pulled forth from the rubble a most beautiful diamond.

Tears flowed uncontrollably in that moment of realization, as if on the wind; he heard the words of that special song that Cole had sung to him so many times before, "We are all coal, we are all coal, a lump or a diamond what e'er is your goal."

To see other works by P.E. Pence, visit: www.pepence.com

Eye of the Nagual

When twins Patch and Yacey discover an ancient amulet, their lives change forever; now hunted by a cabal of bloodthirsty killers, they must travel through the cities and jungles of Central America to learn how to control the mysterious power of the Nagual, an ancient Meso-American shapeshifter, as they seek to fulfill the ancient doomsday prophecies kicked off in the year 2012.

Heart of the Nagual

After the conflict, the twins must continue their Nagual training. Their mother, Maya, traveling with the boys, encounters a dark stranger. The boys notice something pass between them and the familiar look of a Nagual's Eye. No longer a secret, their quest takes them down a dangerous path deep within the dark Nagual's domain.

The Chiasmus Stone

Book 3 of the Nagual series is in progress.

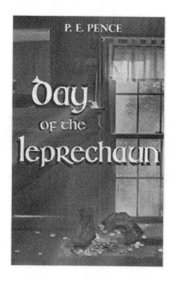

Day of the Leprechaun
Sequel to Christmas Coal

Henry knew he was the cause of the fire that took his best friend's life, but in the ashes, he found a miracle. Henry's little boy faith had believed that the sacrifice made by his friend had provided a miracle, but now, his educated adult self could no longer believe until his day in court, when everyone saw things they couldn't believe. And on the Day of the Leprechaun, they found more than a pot of gold at the rainbow's end.

Frostbite and Little Spark

The elves have lost something important. Will they find it in the trash, or will they find an even bigger problem?!

Coming Soon

The Mother Christmas Series

Becoming Mother Christmas

Mother Christmas and the Light Village

Made in the USA
Columbia, SC
18 November 2024

46380722R10017